This
Buttons Family
book belongs to

- - - - - - - - - - -

- - - - - - - - - - -

Cherry and Charlie and Baby Lou,

We're the Buttons, we're just like you!

And every day there's something new

For Cherry and Charlie and Baby Lou!

First published 2012 by Walker Books Ltd
87 Vauxhall Walk, London SE11 5HJ

10 9 8 7 6 5 4 3 2 1

Text © 2012 Vivian French
Illustrations © 2012 Sue Heap

The right of Vivian French and Sue Heap to be identified as
author and illustrator respectively of this work has been
asserted by them in accordance with the Copyright, Designs
and Patents Act 1988

This book has been typeset in HVD Bodedo

Printed in China

British Library Cataloguing in
Publication Data: a catalogue record
for this book is available from
the British Library

ISBN 978-1-4063-2859-2

www.walker.co.uk

The Buttons Family
Going to the Dentist

Vivian French

illustrated by
Sue Heap

WALKER BOOKS
AND SUBSIDIARIES
LONDON · BOSTON · SYDNEY · AUCKLAND

"Guess what!" said Mum. "You're all booked in at the dentist for a check-up." "Yuck!" Dad made a face. "I hate going to the dentist."

"You always tell us it's fun," said Charlie. "But my tooth hurts," said Dad.

"Why are you here?" Cherry asked a lady in the waiting room. "For a filling," she said, "it won't hurt."

"Buttons family?" called the receptionist.

They all followed Dad
into Mr Ali's room.

"Who's first?" Mr Ali asked.
Dad pushed Baby Lou forward.

"She is!"

Baby Lou opened
her mouth wide.
"WONDERFUL!"
Mr Ali said.
"Let's have
a look."

He picked up a tiny mirror and a little metal instrument. Baby Lou shut her mouth. "Oh!" Mr Ali looked disappointed. "I just wanted to count your teeth."

Baby Lou opened her mouth again. "AHHHHH!" "Brilliant!" Mr Ali said. "Now I'll count your teeth and make sure they're OK."

"Look!" Mr Ali
held up a small
bottle. "Who
wants to
try this?"

"What is it?" Cherry asked. "When you brush your teeth, sometimes you miss bits - this will turn them red."

Cherry's teeth had hardly any red patches, but Charlie's did. Mr Ali showed him in a mirror. "It's called 'plaque'," Mr Ali explained.

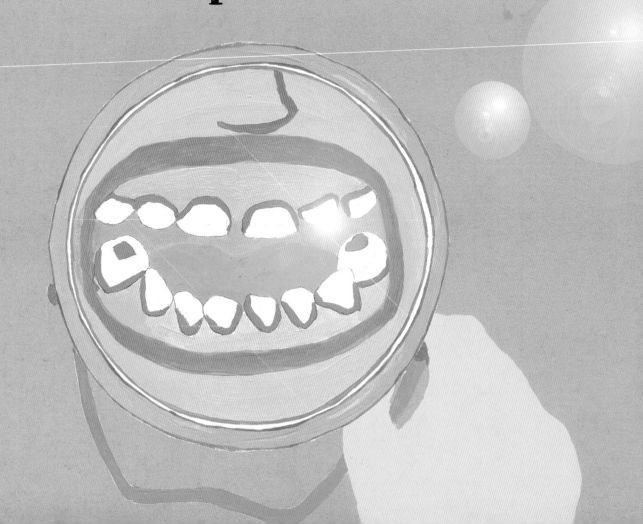

"It's made up of left over bits of food, and it's bad for teeth. Here's a new toothbrush. Let's see if you can clean it off."

Next, Mr Ali looked in Cherry's mouth.

"You've got a tiny hole," he said. "We'll pop some fluoride on it - you'll grow your big teeth before it needs a filling." "Will Dad have fluoride on his sore tooth?" asked Cherry.

"No. Your dad can't grow any more teeth," Mr Ali said.

"I'll take out the bad bit, then put in a nice clean filling. I hope he's as good at opening his mouth as you are!"

When Mr Ali had finished, he gave them each a sticker.

Baby Lou stuck her sticker on Dad's nose. "Thanks, Lou," Dad said. "Will that make my tooth better?" "Mr Ali will," Cherry told him. "He's MAGIC!"

"Now, you all go and sit in the waiting room.

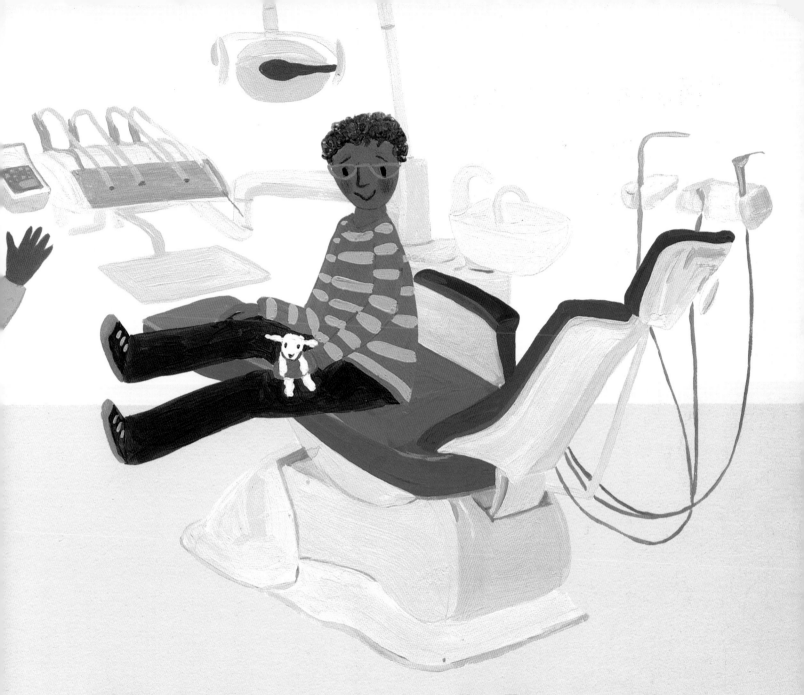

I'll look at your dad's teeth,"
said Mr Ali.

Later, at lunch, Dad was quiet.
"Does your tooth still
hurt?" Cherry asked.
"No," Dad said.
"But Mr Ali says
I must brush my
teeth properly."

"I know how to do that!" said Charlie. "I'll show you. No more fillings for the Buttons family!"

There are six Buttons Family books to collect.
Which ones have you read?

New Shoes

Charlie's shoes are too tight!
He says he doesn't want
new ones, but what do
his toes say?

ISBN 978-1-4063-2855-4

Going to
the Doctor

Cherry's got a nasty cold.
How will Mum persuade
her to go to the doctor?

ISBN 978-1-4063-2857-8

Staying with Gran

Cherry, Charlie and Baby Lou have
never stayed with Gran on their
own before. Will Gran make sure
they feel at home?

ISBN 978-1-4063-2860-8

First Day
at Playschool

It's Cherry's first day
at playschool and she's
feeling a little shy.
How will she settle in?

ISBN 978-1-4063-2856-1

The
Babysitter

Mum and Dad are going out.
What do Cherry, Charlie
and Baby Lou think of the
new babysitter?

ISBN 978-1-4063-2858-5

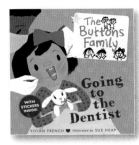

Going to
the Dentist

It's time for the Buttons
to go to the dentist!
How will they get on at
their check-up?

ISBN 978-1-4063-2859-2

Available from all good booksellers